NICKELODEON
SpongeBob SquarePants

Ice-Cream Dreams

Adapted by Nancy Krulik
Illustrated by Heather Martinez
based on the movie written by Derek Drymon, Tim Hill, Steve Hillenburg,
Kent Osborne, Aaron Springer, and Paul Tibbitt

Today was the day SpongeBob had been waiting for all his life.
It was finally opening day at the Krusty Krab 2!

SpongeBob had good reason to be excited. He was sure Mr. Krabs was going to make him manager of the new restaurant. There was no one better for the job.

After all, SpongeBob had been employee of the month at the Krusty Krab 374 times in a row.

"I'm ready," he said proudly. "Promotion!"

SpongeBob spent extra time dressing for work that morning.

"Cleanliness is next to managerliness," he declared as he straightened his square pants and went to work.

The opening of the Krusty Krab 2 was big news in Bikini Bottom.
"Before we begin with the ribbon cutting, I'd like to introduce our
new manager," Mr. Krabs told the TV reporters.
SpongeBob got ready to smile for the cameras.

SpongeBob bounded up to the stage to accept the honor. "People of Bikini Bottom, as the manager of . . . ," he started to say. Then Mr. Krabs whispered something in his ear.

Mr. Krabs *hadn't* said SpongeBob's name. Instead he'd announced, "Please welcome our new manager, *Squidward Tentacles.*"

SpongeBob was shocked. How could Mr. Krabs do this to him?

Mr. Krabs explained that he didn't think SpongeBob was ready for the job. "You're just a kid" he said. "To be a manager, you have to be a man. Otherwise they'd call it a kidager. You understandager?"

SpongeBob did *not* understand. He didn't like being called a kid!

There would be no celebrating tonight. SpongeBob just wanted to go home and be alone in his pineapple.

On his way home, SpongeBob stopped at the Goofy Goober's Party Boat to drown his sorrows. Patrick was there. Patrick loved hearing the Goofy Goober sing.

"Oh, I'm a Goofy Goober, yeah! You're a Goofy Goober, yeah! We're all Goofy Goobers, yeah!" the dancing peanut chanted.

Even the Goofy Goober song wasn't enough to cheer SpongeBob.
Nothing could make him happy.

Until Patrick ordered some ice cream.

A Triple Gooberberry Sunrise, huh? SpongeBob thought. "I guess I could use one of those," he said aloud.

Slurp. Splatter. Yum. SpongeBob gulped down a whole sundae. "That hit the spot. I'm feeling better already."

Once SpongeBob got started eating Triple Gooberberry Sunrises, he couldn't stop. Neither could Patrick.

Chomp, chomp. Slurp, slurp.
In a matter of seconds, they'd
eaten two more. And they
weren't finished yet!

"Woohoo," SpongeBob called out. "Waaaiter!" He held up two fingers.

"Why do I always get the goofy ones?" the waiter wondered aloud as he made two more Triple Gooberberry Sunrises.

All that ice cream was making SpongeBob really silly.

"This one goes out to my two bestest friends in the whole world," SpongeBob announced. "Patrick, and this peanut guy. It's a little song called . . .

"*Waaaaii-terrrrrrrrr!*" SpongeBob and Patrick sang together.

The waiter kept the Triple Gooberberry Sunrises coming all night long . . . until SpongeBob and Patrick fell asleep.

The first thing SpongeBob wanted when he woke up in the morning was a Double Fudge Spinny. A Triple Gooberberry Sunrise just didn't seem like a breakfast food.

After eating his sundae SpongeBob headed off for another day of work at the Krusty Krab. The whole way there he thought about how angry he was at Mr. Krabs for giving the manager job to Squidward.

But Mr. Krabs had bigger troubles on his mind. King Neptune had paid him a visit. He believed Mr. Krabs had stolen his crown and sold it to Shell City. It wasn't true, of course. But King Neptune didn't care. He was ready to cook Mr. Krabs. . . .

Unless someone was man enough to go to the dreaded Shell City, rescue the crown, and find out who the real thief was.

SpongeBob was the first to volunteer. He would save Mr. Krabs's life.

"The road to Shell City is the most dangerous journey of all," the king warned. "What chance would you have? You're just a kid."

"I know I can do it!" SpongeBob vowed. "Let's go get that crown, Pat!" SpongeBob knew in his spongy heart that he could be a brave man—as in manager!